Thomas

 **A GOLDEN BOOK • NEW YORK**

rhcbooks.com
Educators and librarians, for a variety of teaching tools, visit us at RHTeachersLibrarians.com
ISBN 978-0-307-97659-8 (trade)
MANUFACTURED IN CHINA
10 9 8 7 6 5 4 3 2 1
2021 Edition

Based on the Marvel comic book series Spider-Man
Adapted by Frank Berrios
Illustrated by Francesco Legramandi and Andrea Cagol

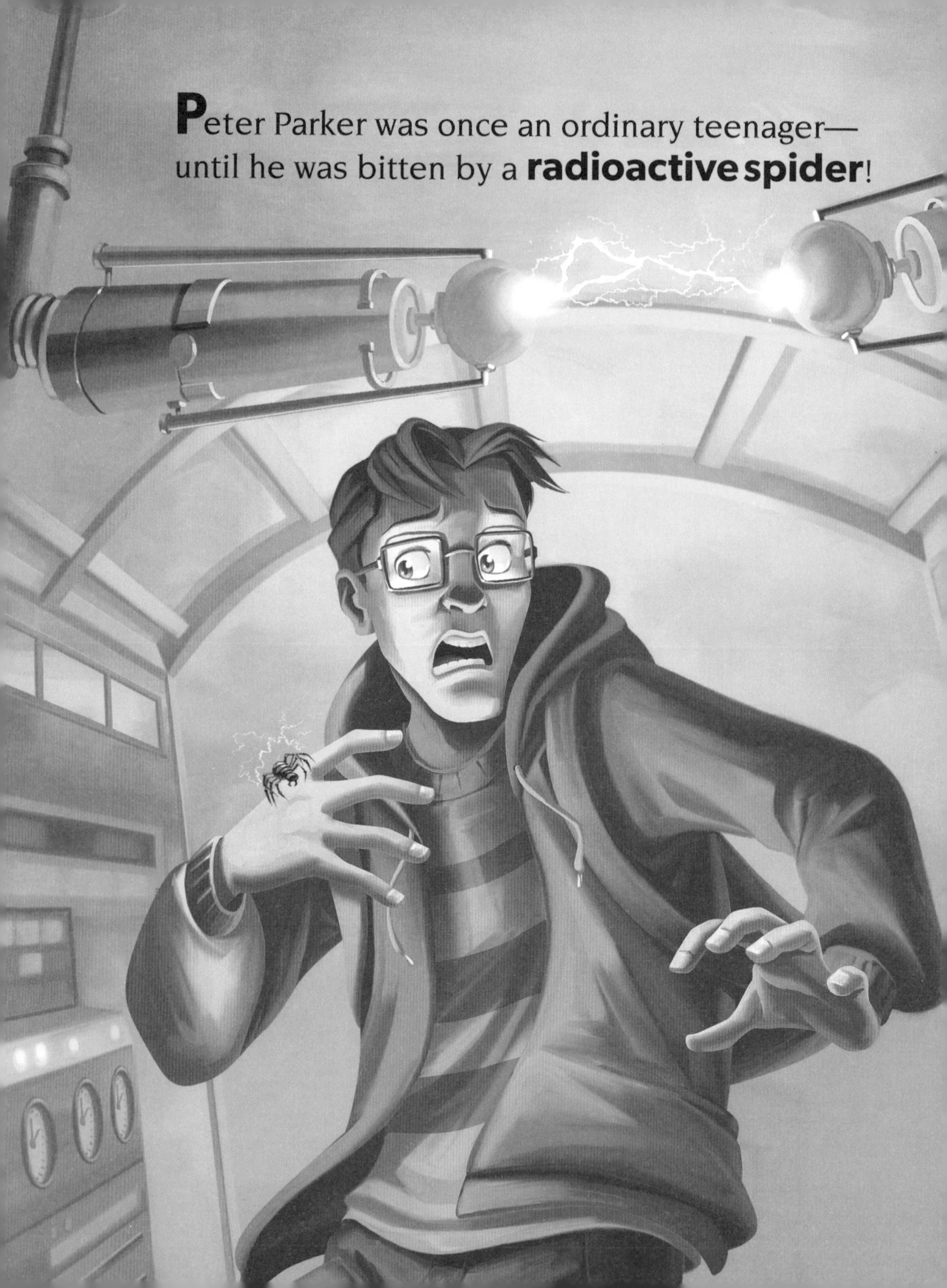

Peter Parker was once an ordinary teenager— until he was bitten by a **radioactive spider**!

The bite gave Peter super strength and the amazing ability to cling to walls—just like a man-sized spider. So Peter Parker decided to become the super hero called **Spider-Man**!

Peter Parker created a costume to wear so that no one would know he was really Spider-Man.

Peter also invented **web shooters** that allowed him to swing through the city from building to building.

Spider-Man can use his web shooters in many ways.

He can make a shield for protection or a parachute to float safely to the ground.

And Spider-Man can use his webs
to stop bad guys in their tracks!

Spider-Man also has a "spider sense," which alerts him to danger. When his **spidey-sense** starts tingling, Spider-Man knows that trouble is nearby!

Some people, such as J. Jonah Jameson, publisher of the newspaper the *Daily Bugle*, think Spider-Man is a menace. They don't trust him because he wears a mask to hide his face.

But most people know that Spider-Man is really a **hero**!

No trouble is too big—or too small—for Spider-Man to handle!

Because he fights bad guys, Spider-Man has made lots of enemies. **Supervillains** are always looking for a way to get rid of the Wall-Crawler!

The Vulture wears a winged costume that doubles his strength and gives him the ability to fly. Whenever this bad bird soars into town, he causes trouble for Spider-Man!

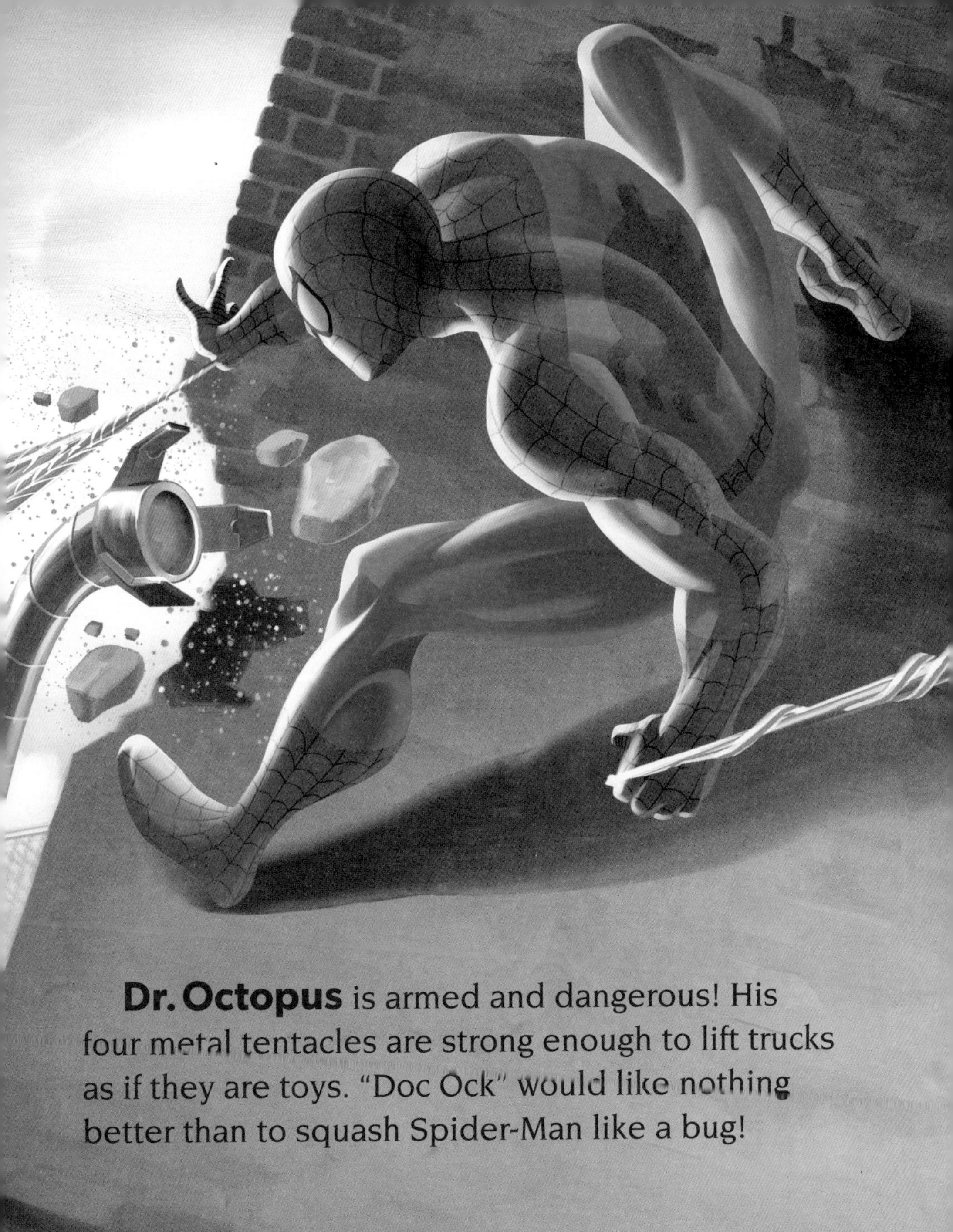

Dr. Octopus is armed and dangerous! His four metal tentacles are strong enough to lift trucks as if they are toys. "Doc Ock" would like nothing better than to squash Spider-Man like a bug!

The Sandman is made of living sand! He can slip through the smallest cracks or make his fist rock-hard to smash his enemies. But Spider-Man thinks fast and always cleans the floor with this gritty thug!

The Lizard was once a doctor—but his research with lizards turned him into a half-man, half-reptile monster. Spider-Man needs all his amazing powers to escape the Lizard's whipping tail and sharp claws!

The Green Goblin commits crimes with a rocket-powered glider and a bag full of explosive pumpkin bombs. The Goblin's gloves can fire powerful electric shocks, so Spider-Man has to move fast when he faces this frightful fiend!

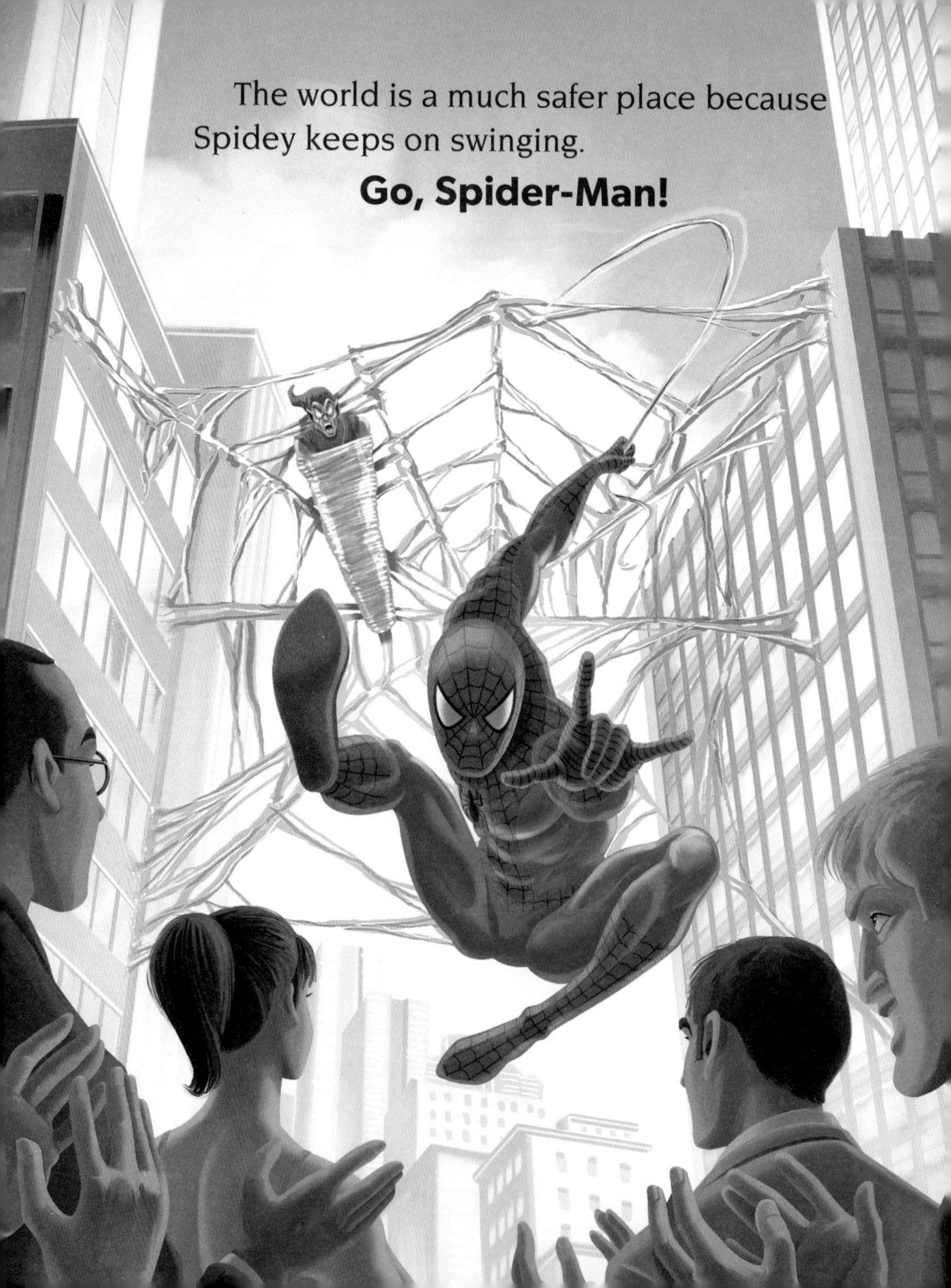

The world is a much safer place because Spidey keeps on swinging.

Go, Spider-Man!

The Big Freeze

Based on the Marvel comic book series Spider-Man
Adapted by Billy Wrecks
Illustrated by Michael Borkowski and Michael Atiyeh

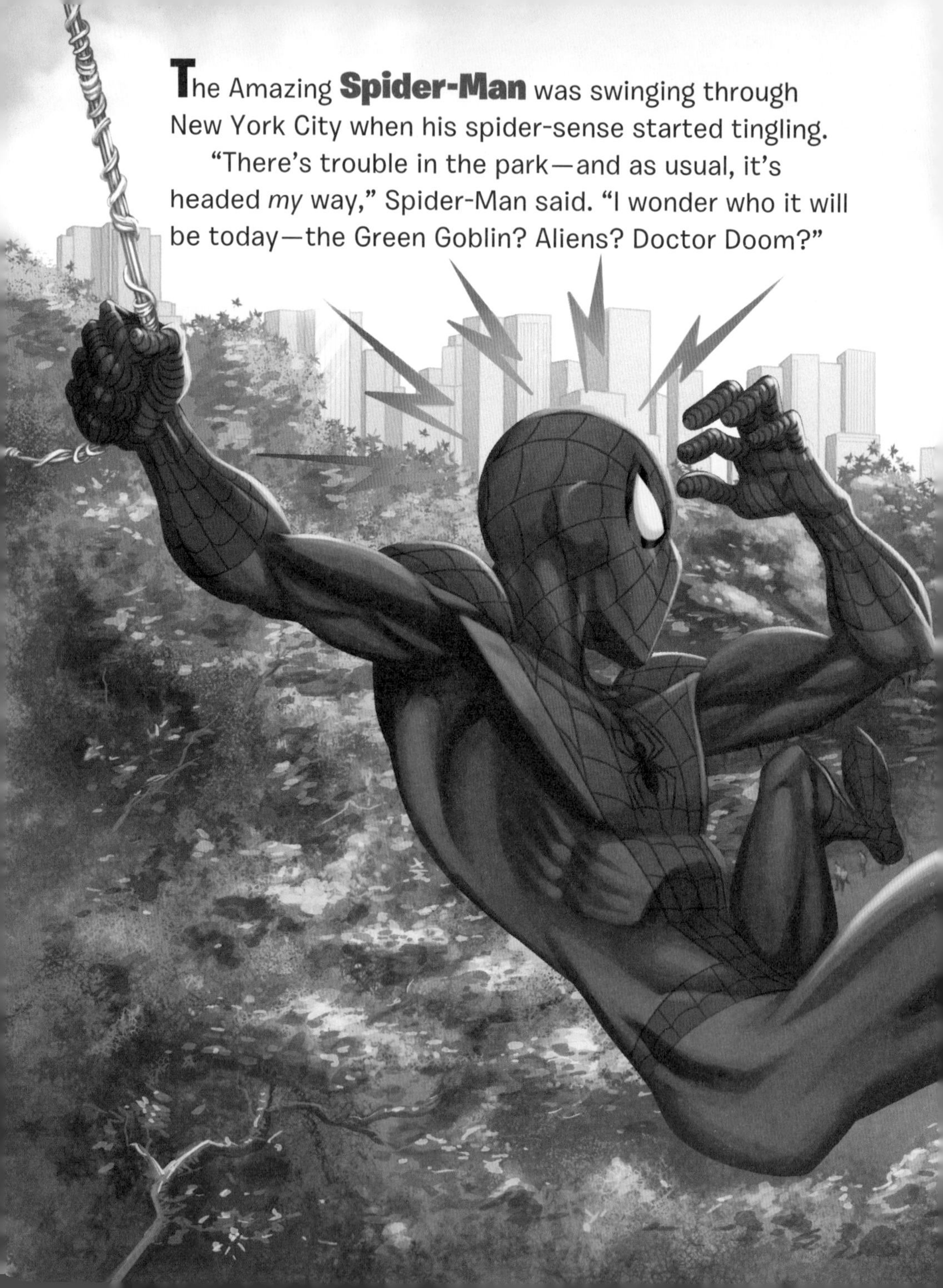

The Amazing **Spider-Man** was swinging through New York City when his spider-sense started tingling.

"There's trouble in the park—and as usual, it's headed *my* way," Spider-Man said. "I wonder who it will be today—the Green Goblin? Aliens? Doctor Doom?"

Spider-Man jumped out of the way as a huge green blur hurtled past him.

Now I know there's trouble! Spider-Man thought.

The big green blur smashed into the street. It was the Incredible **Hulk**.

"Now Hulk is angry," the green giant growled. "Make Hulk want to **SMASH!**"

"Whoa, big fella. What happened?" Spider-Man asked.

"Big blue men came through hole in the sky," Hulk snarled. "Blue men look for Hulk's friend, blond hair."

"Blue men? Blond hair? What are you talking about?" Spider-Man replied as enormous shadows loomed over them. "And why is it getting dark? Uh-oh."

Spider-Man looked up. Three fierce **Frost Giants** from the distant realm of Asgard towered above them.

"We are looking for Thor," boomed the leader of the Frost Giants—who was also the biggest. "And I will cover this city with ice and snow until he faces us!"

Suddenly, a repulsor ray blasted one of the Frost Giants.
It was—

Iron Man!

"Thor is on the way," Iron Man warned the Frost Giants. "But until he gets here, you will just have to deal with . . .

. . . us!”

As the biggest Frost Giant continued to summon more snow, Iron Man, Spider-Man, and Hulk bravely fought the foes. But the Frost Giants were very big and very strong!

"I thought the bigger they were, the harder they fell!" Spider-Man joked.

"Less talk. More SMASH, Bug Man!" Hulk growled.

"Brrr," Spider-Man said, covering the biggest Frost Giant with his web. "You better wrap up before you catch a cold."

“Let’s lead the Frost Giants back to the park, where they won’t cause as much damage,” Iron Man suggested.

“Good idea, Shell Head,” Spider-Man replied. “Hulk said something about a hole in the sky. Maybe it’s the portal they came through.”

Suddenly, thunder rumbled and lightning flashed!
"Laufey!" **Thor** roared at the biggest Frost Giant. "What is the meaning of this?"

"The last time we met, on that snowy battlefield, you were victorious," Laufey snarled. "I promised to get even. And today I shall!"

Without warning, Laufey hurled a big, frosty snowball at Thor with blinding speed!

Thor swung his mighty hammer and smashed the snowball. Ice splattered everywhere!

"Gotcha!" Laufey roared gleefully. Then all three Frost Giants dashed for the open portal in the sky.

"HA! HA!" Thor laughed heartily. "Well struck, Frost Giants! But this time I have my friends. Join me, heroes!"

The heroes quickly jumped into the snowball fight with the Frost Giants. Even the people of New York helped!

Thor chased the Frost Giants back to their portal. As it closed behind them, everyone cheered!

“The Frost Giants are gone, but the city is still covered in snow,” Spider-Man said to Hulk and Iron Man. “I guess there’s only one thing to do—**DUCK!**”

Trapped by the Green Goblin!

Based on the Marvel comic book series Spider-Man
Adapted by Frank Berrios
Illustrated by Francesco Legramandi and Andrea Cagol

OSCOR

Late one night, the super hero **Spider-Man** saw some men robbing a warehouse.

"Isn't it a little late to be shopping?" Spider-Man asked as he swung down on them.

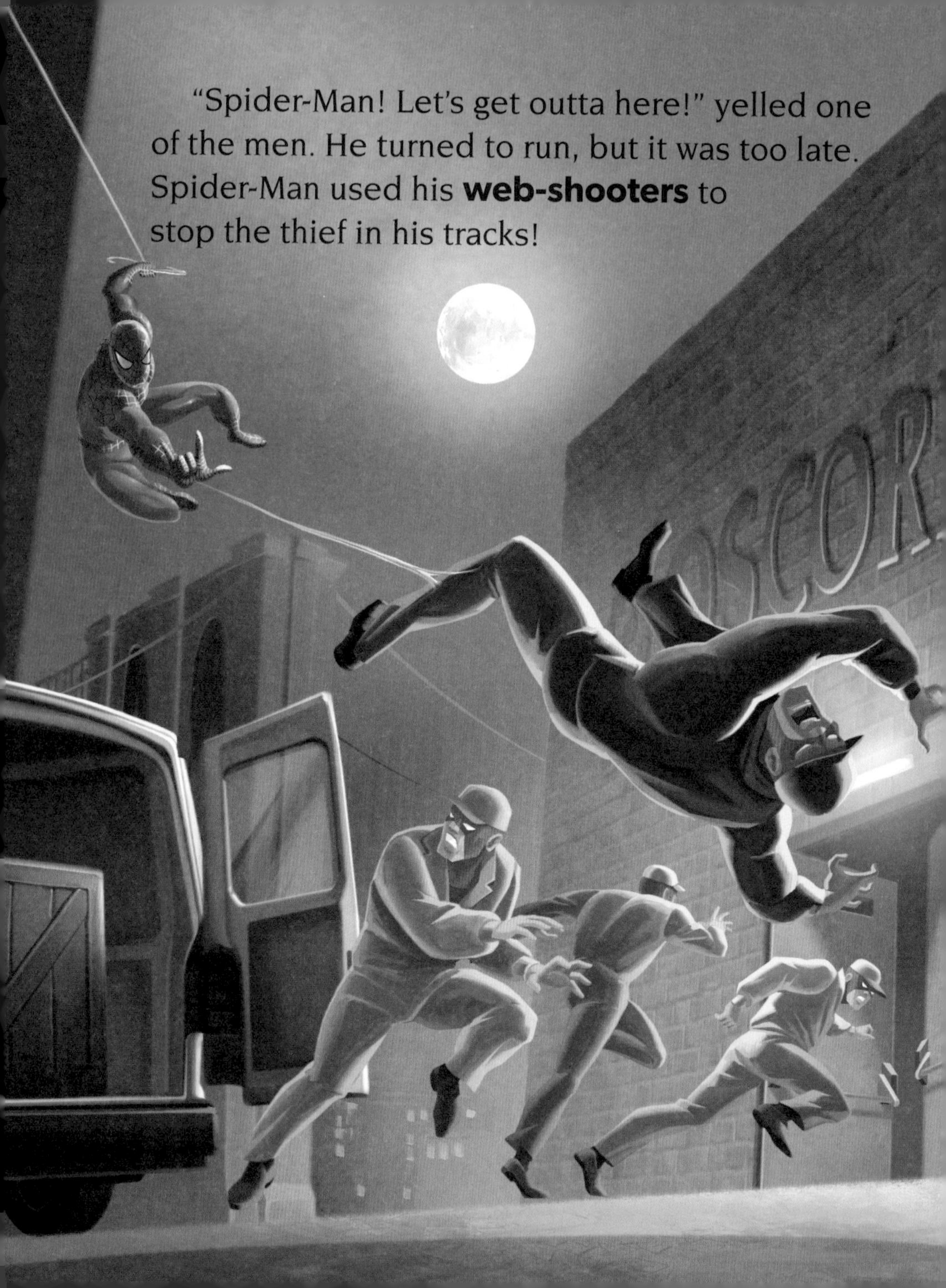

"Spider-Man! Let's get outta here!" yelled one of the men. He turned to run, but it was too late. Spider-Man used his **web-shooters** to stop the thief in his tracks!

Spider-Man followed the thieves into the warehouse.

In the dark building, his **spider-sense** started to tingle—there was danger ahead!

Suddenly, the lights snapped on. It was a trap! The villain known as the **GREEN GOBLIN** laughed.

"All this for me?" Spider-Man joked. "And it's not even my birthday!"

"I will make you wish you had never been born!" replied the Goblin. "Now crush him!"

One of the Goblin's thugs grabbed Spider-Man with his oversized mechanical hands and **SQUEEZED!**

"Didn't your mother tell you to keep your hands to yourself?" Spider-Man said, bending the thug's mechanical arms out of shape.

Spider-Man swung through the air. He landed on the back of a thug wearing a jet pack.

"Sorry to drop in on you like this," Spider-Man said, ripping out the jet pack's wires.

“Happy landings!” said Spider-Man as the thug wearing the jet pack crashed into the oncoming steamroller. **KA-BOOM!**

“Now it’s just you and me, Goblin,” said Spider-Man.

“Those fools failed to defeat you, but I won’t,” snarled the Green Goblin.

"Take this!" the Green Goblin yelled. He threw a handful of **pumpkin bombs** at Spider-Man.

The wall-crawler flipped out of harm's way as the bombs exploded around him.

"Sorry, Goblin—you just don't blow me away!" said Spider-Man. But suddenly, the Green Goblin zapped him with a bolt of electricity!

Spider-Man fell into a cage with fast-moving bars. He ducked and dodged the bars, but they were closing in. Soon he'd be trapped!

"You're the one who belongs behind bars," Spider-Man said, "not me." With all his strength, he smashed his way out of the cage!

"Will none of my traps hold you?" the shocked Green Goblin roared at the wall-crawler.

"You may have escaped, but you will never capture me!" the villain vowed, throwing razor-sharp bat blades as he escaped on his **Goblin glider**. "I will return to destroy you."

“Do you really think you can beat the one and only Spider-Man with a bunch of high-tech toys?” asked the super hero.

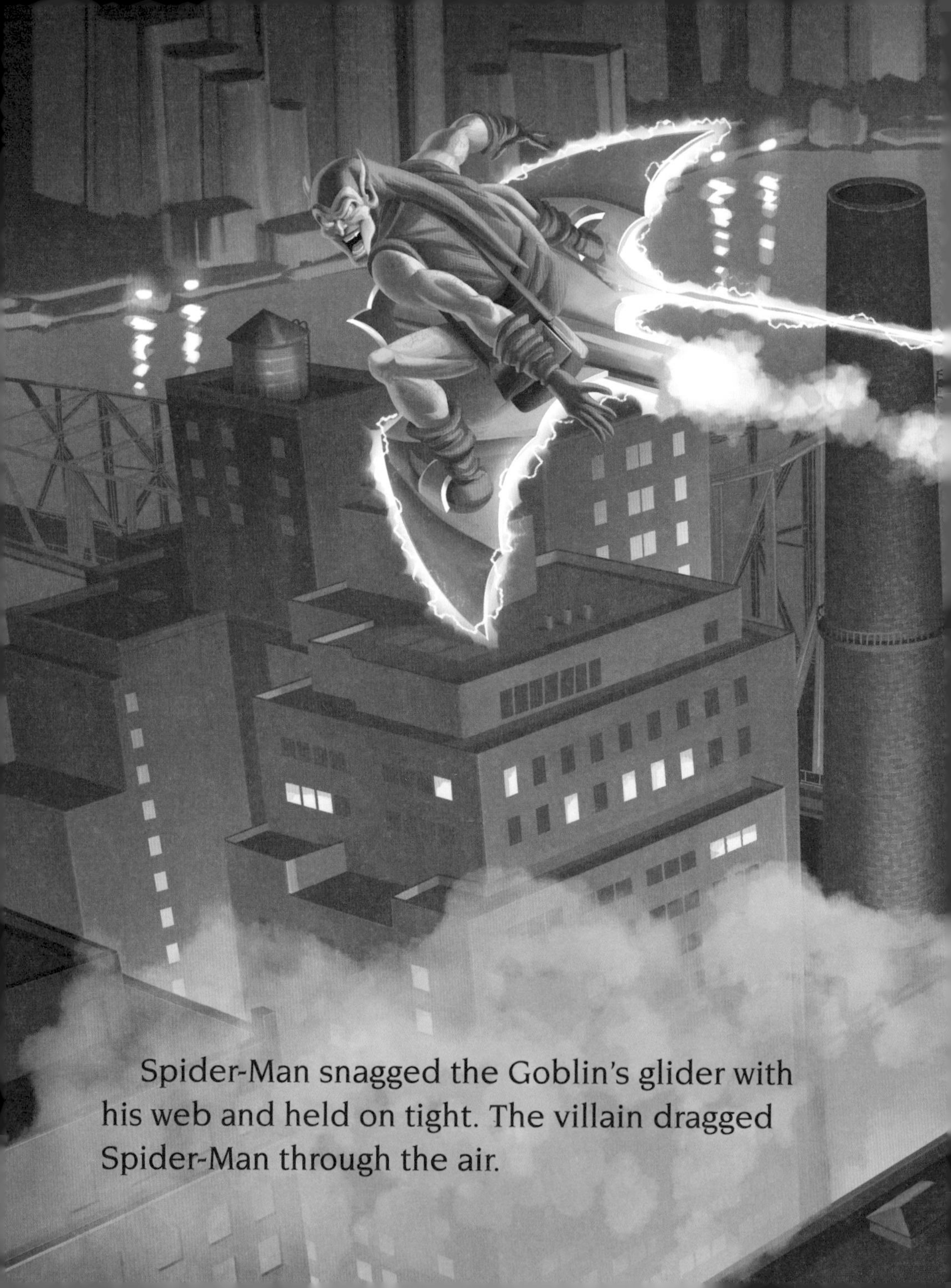

Spider-Man snagged the Goblin's glider with his web and held on tight. The villain dragged Spider-Man through the air.

"Get off, you annoying insect!" yelled the Goblin. He sent a bolt of electricity through the hero's web.

The Green Goblin laughed and circled back to make sure the hero was done for. Suddenly, the web-slinger moved with incredible speed.

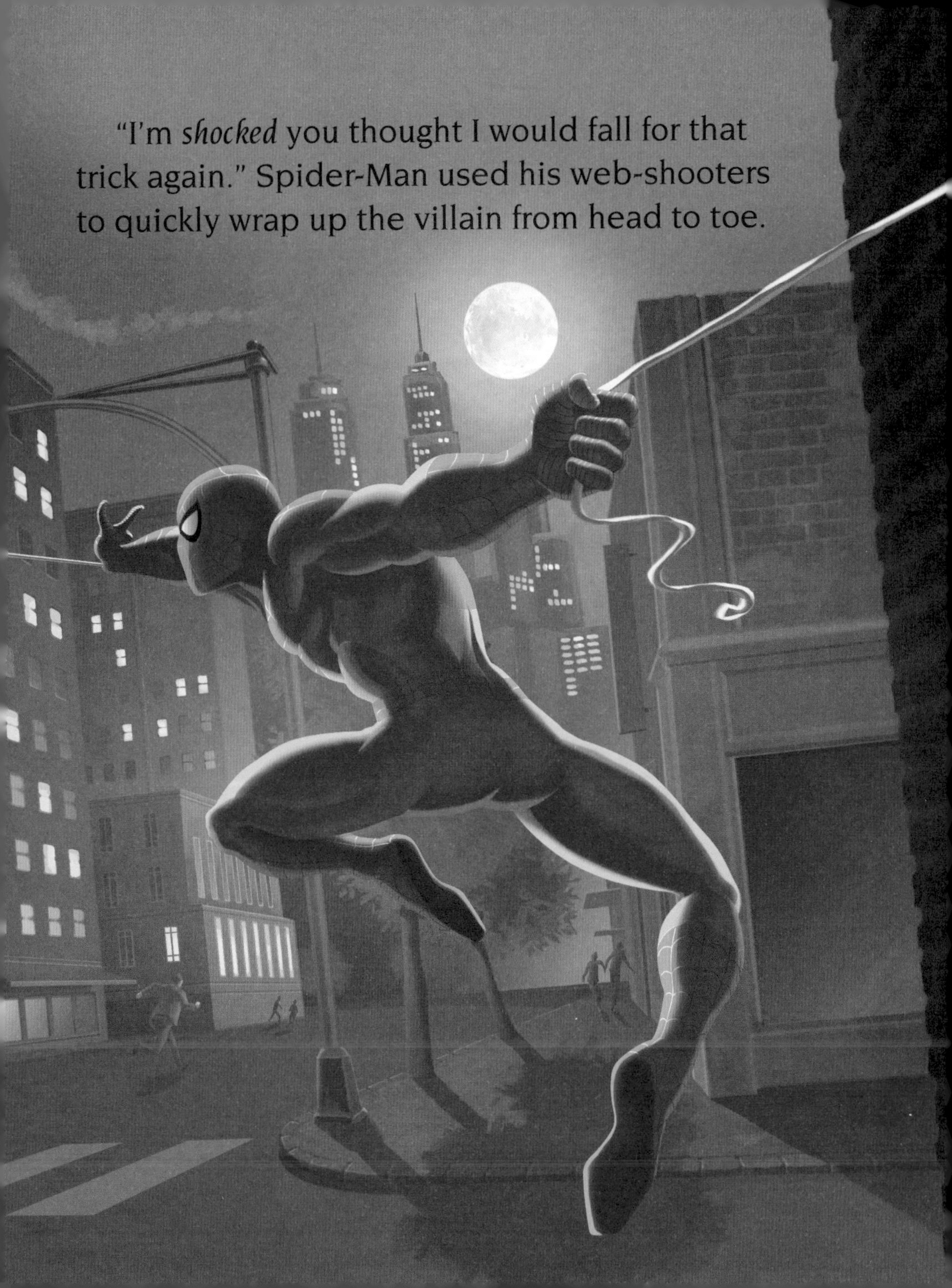

"I'm *shocked* you thought I would fall for that trick again." Spider-Man used his web-shooters to quickly wrap up the villain from head to toe.

"There won't be any more tricks or treats for you," the hero told the villain, "unless there's Halloween in jail!"

Then your friendly neighborhood Spider-Man swung off in search of his next adventure.